NO MORE BATHS

Brock Cole

A Sunburst Book
Farrar, Straus and Giroux

NO MORE BATHS

for Susan

One day when Jessie McWhistle came in for lunch, her dad gave her a kiss on the cheek and said, "Why, I believe you have a stalk of corn growing out of your ear, Jessie!"

"Pay no attention to him," said her big brother, Bert. "You don't have any corn growing out of your ears. It isn't anything but a little bit of grass."

That made Jessie mad.

"You're teasing me," she said. "It's not right to give somebody a kiss just so you can look in their ears. I'm going to tell Mom."

But her mom said that what she needed was a nice hot bath, and she went off to fill the tub.

When Jessie heard the water running into the tub, she made up her mind to leave home.

"I'm running away!" she said. "Don't think I'm ever coming back, because I've got friends and none of them ever has to take a bath in the middle of the day."

"Send us a postcard!" said her brother, Bert.

"Now listen here, young lady . . ." said her dad.

But Jessie didn't listen.

She ran out the back door and down the
path through the trees along the river.

She hadn't gone far when she came to the sandy place where the sun shone all day long on the pigweed and pricker bushes.

There was Mrs. Chicken, scratching in the sand and clucking to herself.

"Hello, Jessie," said Mrs. Chicken. "Where are you off to?"

"I've run away from home, Mrs. Chicken. I'm not going back because they make you take baths even in the middle of the day."

"That's terrible," said Mrs. Chicken. "Why don't you come and live with me and be a chicken?"

"I'd like that," said Jessie. "Will you show me how?"

"I'd be glad to," said Mrs. Chicken. "The first thing I'll show you is how to frazzle."

"How do you do that?" asked Jessie.

"Watch me, Jessie," said Mrs. Chicken. "You find a nice dusty spot in the sun and squoosh down and ruffle up and shake sand all over your feathers."

Mrs. Chicken shook the sand out of her feathers like dust from a dust mop.

It looked easy, so Jessie threw some sand in her hair and down the back of her neck.

But no matter how she shook herself . . .

she couldn't get the sand out.

She itched and scratched all over.

"Whooee," said Jessie. "How often does a chicken have to frazzle anyway? Just once to join, or is it something more regular than that?"

"What did you say?" said Mrs. Chicken. "Just once? Chickens love to frazzle, Jessie. A chicken has to frazzle to keep clean."

"I'm afraid I don't have the talent," said Jessie.

"Don't let it fret you," said Mrs. Chicken. "Not just anybody can be a chicken. Why, frazzling is child's play compared to laying eggs."

So Jessie said goodbye and went off down the path along the river through the trees.

She hadn't gone far when she came to the old deserted mill. Who was sunning herself on the stone doorstep but Mrs. Cat?

"Hello, Mrs. Cat," said Jessie.
"Hello, Jessica," said Mrs. Cat.
"Where are you off to?"

"I've run away from home, Mrs. Cat, and I'm not ever going back because they make you take baths even in the middle of the day."

"Baths?" said Mrs. Cat. "Cats never take baths."

"Really?" said Jessie. "Do you think I could be a cat?"

"I don't know," said Mrs. Cat. "I think you should spruce up a bit before we decide.

"Now watch closely. First you lick your paw, and brush around your eyes and behind your ears . . ."

"Come on, now," said Mrs. Cat. "Lick your paw. Brush hard."

Jessie tried. She licked the palm of her hand and rubbed her nose and behind her ears as hard as she could.

But her hair didn't look clean and shiny like Mrs. Cat's. It was sticky and tangled.

"Well," sighed Mrs. Cat, "I'm afraid you aren't meant to be a cat. But not just anybody can be a cat. Not just anybody, you understand . . .

can catch MICE!"

So Jessie McWhistle said goodbye and walked off down the path through the trees along the river.

She hadn't gone far when she met Mrs. Pig.

"Hello, Mrs. Pig," said Jessie.

"Howdy-do, Jessie," said Mrs. Pig. "Where are you off to?"

"I've run away from home, Mrs. Pig, and I'm not ever going back because they make you take baths even in the middle of the day."

"What's a bath?" asked Mrs. Pig.

"A bath?" said Jessie. "Why, that's when they throw you in a tub of boiling water and rub soap in your eyes."

"Woof!" said Mrs. Pig. "That sounds terrible. Why don't you come and live with me and be a pig?"

"I'd like that," said Jessie. "But is it hard to be a pig?"

"Pshaw!" said Mrs. Pig. "Being a pig is the easiest and grandest thing in the world."

So Jessie went off down the path with Mrs. Pig.

They hadn't gone far when they came to a marshy place where a spring dribbled down and the mosquitoes hummed and sang.

Mrs. Pig plowed into the biggest puddle she could find and sat down in the soft mud.

"Come on in, Jessie," she called. "I'll show you how to get a nice even coat of mud. It will keep you cool."

Mrs. Pig looked so comfortable that
Jessie walked right in and sat down.

It did feel nice and cool.

"What do pigs do now?" asked Jessie.

"Well," said Mrs. Pig, "they generally take a nap, and then go root for acorns."

Mrs. Pig's voice began to get sleepy, and she sighed dreamily.

"And then we'll go and scratch on the fence for a while, and then we'll go have some more acorns."

Jessie began to feel wet and cold.

She thought about peanut-butter sandwiches and the smell of clean sheets hanging on the line in the sun.

After a minute she got up.

"Well," she said, "I can see that being a pig is a fine thing, but I don't think I'll start today."

Mrs. Pig didn't say anything. She was fast asleep.

Jessie walked up the path through the trees toward her own house.

On her way she met her dad, who was bringing in the cows.

"Welcome home, stranger," he said. "I'm glad you've decided to live with us for a while."

But Jessie didn't say one word.

Her brother, Bert, was peeling potatoes in the kitchen.

"My goodness!" he said. "You look like you fell in the hog wallow."

Jessie still didn't say one word.

She went upstairs to the bathroom and turned on the water in the tub and took off her clothes. Then she got in the tub.

"Will you look at your scalp!" said her mother, who came in to help her wash her hair. "It looks as if someone has been throwing in sand by the handful!"

When she was all clean, her mom wrapped her up in a big fluffy towel and gave her a hug.

"There now," she said. "There are worse things than taking a bath, aren't there?"

Jessie McWhistle knew the answer to that one.

"Nope," she said.

And that's that.